ORIOLE PARK BRANCH
DATE DUE   5-02

APR 2 6 2003			
AUG 0 2 2003			

ARACHNE SPEAKS

ARACHNE SPEAKS

by Kate Hovey

with paintings by
Blair Drawson

Margaret K. McElderry Books

NEW YORK

LONDON

TORONTO

SYDNEY

SINGAPORE

Margaret K. McElderry Books
An imprint of Simon & Schuster Children's Publishing Division
1230 Avenue of the Americas
New York, NY 10020

Book design by Ann Bobco
The text of this book is set in Deepdene.
The illustrations are rendered in acrylic paints.

Printed in Hong Kong
2 4 6 8 10 9 7 5 3 1

Library of Congress Cataloging-in-Publication Data
Hovey, Kate. Arachne speaks / Kate Hovey ; with paintings by Blair Drawson.–1st ed.   p.   cm.
Summary: A poem about Arachne, who challenged the goddess Athena
to a weaving contest and was changed into a spider.
ISBN 0-689-82901-9
1. Arachne (Greek mythology)-Juvenile poetry. 2. Children's poetry, American.
[1. Arachne (Greek mythology)-Poetry. 2. Mythology, Greek-Poetry.
3. American poetry.] I. Drawson, Blair, ill. II. Title.
PS3558.O8749 A88 2000
811'.54-dc21   99-046926

FIRST
EDITION

To Mom

In memory of
William Gifford "Wild Bill" Hovey

In celebration of
a tapestry richly woven
—K. H.

For my beloved aunt, Irene Carter McLean,
who taught me to be Curious about Everything.
—B. D.

Orb weavers!
Weavers of tangled nets!
All eight-legged ones
whose spinnerets
weave the dome,
funnel and sheet,
who shuttle silk
between combed feet:
Leave behind
your tattered lairs
above the hearth,
beneath the stairs,
in gardens and meadows,
by rivers and streams.
Arise—unravel
your web of dreams!
    Begin our tapestry again;
    cover the earth from end to end!

Cast to the four winds
my story's thread—
let truth spread
like gossamer from your abdomens
across the fields of time!
Children, weave it well;
your silk will tell
a tale of punishment and crime,
of a goddess's black deed
by which you are bound
to spin forever, round and round.
So it was decreed
long ago in Maeonia, my home,
where I first turned
a spindle and learned
the weaver's art. I could comb
the coarsest wool into soft clouds,
spinning it tight.
My fingers were swift and light.
I drew admiring crowds
and proud Athena's wrath;

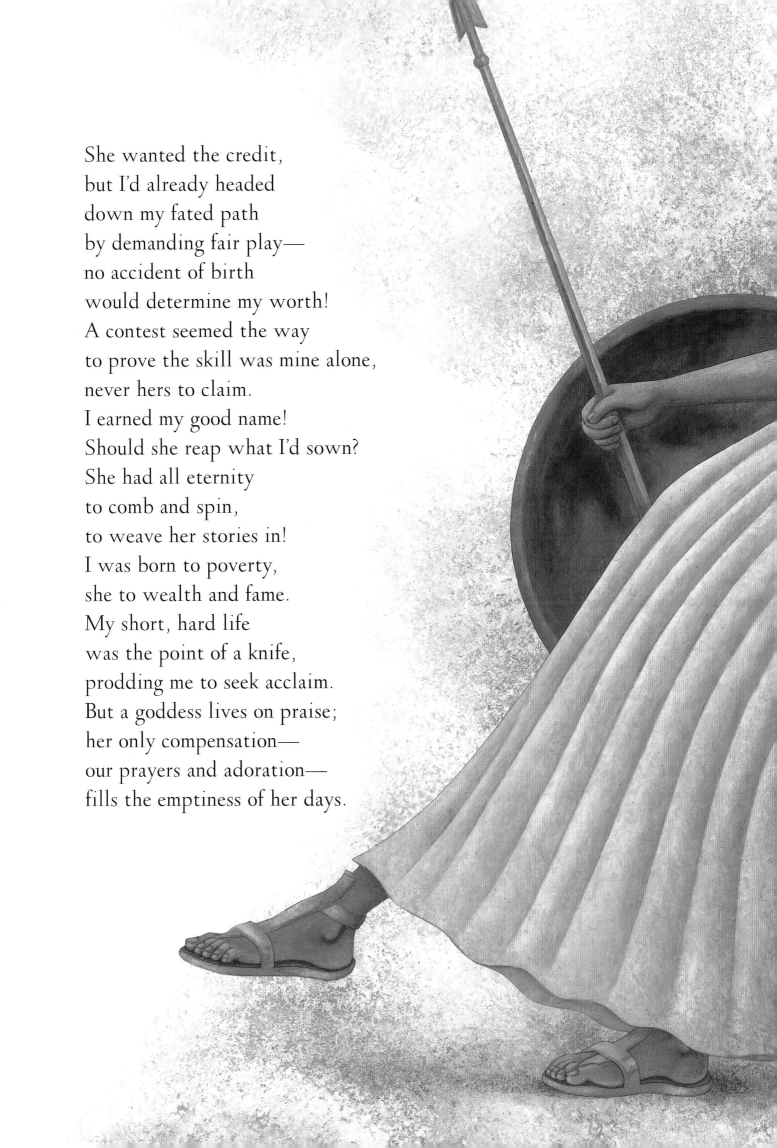

She wanted the credit,
but I'd already headed
down my fated path
by demanding fair play—
no accident of birth
would determine my worth!
A contest seemed the way
to prove the skill was mine alone,
never hers to claim.
I earned my good name!
Should she reap what I'd sown?
She had all eternity
to comb and spin,
to weave her stories in!
I was born to poverty,
she to wealth and fame.
My short, hard life
was the point of a knife,
prodding me to seek acclaim.
But a goddess lives on praise;
her only compensation—
our prayers and adoration—
fills the emptiness of her days.

How could I let it stand,
this challenge to my command?
I, daughter of Zeus,
must suffer such abuse?
I was mocked, maligned—
I should have struck her blind—
but something held me back,
made me take a gentle tack;
after all, a mother grants
her wayward child a second chance,
and whom but a goddess could she defy?
She was as motherless as I!
"She'll learn," I thought, "to bend her knee
and yield to my authority."

She sniffed my rising fame like smoke
ascending from the sacrifice,
more pleasing than a fragrant spice.
I shook my fist and spoke:
"These parasites to whom we pray—
if we'd refuse to feed
their never-ending need,
they'd simply waste away!"
Murmuring, the troubled crowd
retreated from my loom.
"Your words will spell your doom!"
a strange voice called aloud.
Disguised as a hobbling crone
my rival finally came,
warning me to quit the game.
"Offer prayers," she croaked. *"Atone!*
Make no further offense.
Take my advice
or pay the price
for your impertinence!"

"Old woman," I laughed,
"You've lived too long—
 your mind is gone!
 Why would I let my craft
 bring honor to another?
 Since childhood I've been on my own,
 toiling endless hours alone.
 No nimble-fingered mother
 taught me to twist this thread!
 No goddess stood by me!
 My spindle kept me company,
 twirling 'til my fingers bled.
 So pray, if you choose.
 As for me, I've vowed
 to keep my head unbowed!
 Athena's just afraid to lose;
 why doesn't she appear?
 We should settle this—
 what cowardice!"
 The old hag boomed,
 "She's here!"

Pallas cast her cane aside;
towering nearly eight feet tall,
she let her spear and helmet fall
and stared at me, wild-eyed.
I feel them even now,
burning like a brand—
Athena's eternal reprimand—
those eyes blazing in a brow
as broad as a hero's shield.
I turned bright red
from feet to head;
Still, I refused to yield.

Feet apart, shoulders square,
chin thrust boldly in the air;
defiant to the end—
this sapling would not bend!
I threw down my disguise,
staring deep into her eyes,
and wondered, drawing nearer,
was I gazing in a mirror?

While others crouched in fear,
Pallas waved her hand
in a silent command
and made a great loom appear.
She held out fine thread
for the crowd to admire:
Royal purples from Tyre,
spun gold burnished with red.
I ignored the precious strands
to keep my rage controlled—
who needed her gold?
But Father's wretched hands
flashed before my eyes,
stained and bent
from many years spent
stirring hot vats of dyes.
As I watched the vision slowly ebb,
my trembling fingers wound
the thread he colored round and round
to make a sturdy web.
I bound it swiftly to the beam;
My plan was sketched,
the fine warp stretched.
I moved in a dream.

Over and back, my hands kept pace
with the rhythm of warp and weft,
drawing a strand from right to left,
combing it into place,
my shuttle slipping with ease
between thin walls of thread,
navigating the narrow shed
like a boat on familiar seas.
Over and back again it flew:
first Zeus, disguised as a bull,
woven in white lamb's wool,
swam deep in Ionian blue.
Europa gripped his golden horn,
her wide doe-eyes
stitched sideways in surprise.
Her chiton, loosely worn,
billowed on my artful breeze.
Foaming the waves, it seemed to stir
her fragrance of rose and myrrh
as it silvered the shoreline trees.

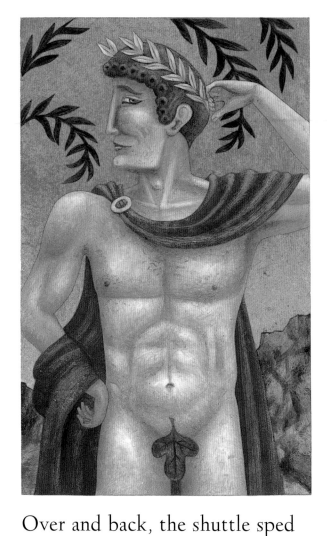

Over and back, the shuttle sped
through glorious but cruel scenes,
unmasking more immortal fiends,
each evildoer spread
across my loom for all to see:
Apollo (stitched in silk),
Poseidon and his ilk,
Dionysus with Erigone.
Embroidered leaves and vines
clinging to the narrow hem
formed a wreath, surrounding them.
When the dark, tangled lines,
drawn over and back, were done,
I knew by their faces
my web of disgraces
had easily won.

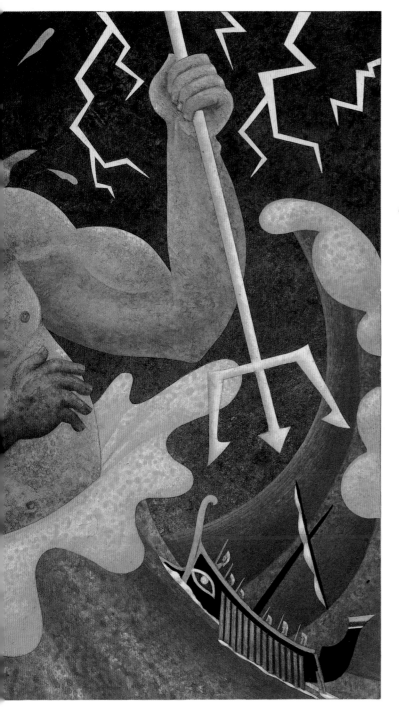

*Rash child, what have
you wrought?
What madness could
have brought
your talents to this end?
Great are the powers you offend!*

Before a storm, the ground
seems pressed by an awful weight—
stillness none can penetrate.
All breath is held; no single sound
escapes a living thing.
No leaf is stirred,
no bee, no bird
dares to beat its wing.
So it was that final hour
before Athena's blast;
A silence unsurpassed
mingled with the sun's power
to forge a leaden heat
no shade could ease.
The crowd sank to its knees,
writhing at Athena's feet
like serpents in the nest.
I grew too weak
to move or speak;
My heart, a hammer in my breast.
As I struggled to stand,
voiceless trees
shuddered. A strong breeze
gripped me with an icy hand.

Athena, loud as thunder,
shouted, *"Boreas, cold one—*
tear this heat from the sun!
Turn it aside, plow under
the wickedness she's sown
now, before it spreads!
Undo these evil threads!
Arachne must atone!"
The North Wind's angry gale
howled as it blew;
my masterpiece ripped in two.
It flapped like a tattered sail
as Boreas tore it from the beam,
strewing colors on the ground.
I watched them swirl around
like dry leaves on a stream.

A crash split the air.
Armor flashed through deepening gloom;
Athena wrecked my loom,
hurling splinters everywhere.
She aimed her shuttle at my head.
I felt a numbing blow,
the sudden flow
of warmth, where it bled
bright rivers down my face,
forming dark pools on the floor.
Athena—three times more—
struck that same broken place
'til white bone showed
beneath the red.
I staggered to my feet—fled
to where a rope was stowed.

Pulling the supple coils free,
my tortured mind began
devising its dark plan
to end Athena's tyranny.
I thought, "If I must die,
then let it be by choice!"
Hearing her angry voice,
I stumbled toward a nearby tree,
fastened the rope, drew it tight,
dangled just above the ground,
made one soft, strangled sound
as everything went white.

Spin round! Spin round!
Too late to cut you down!
Too proud, too strong, too clever—
now you must spin forever.
Hang at MY command.
Your rope, this silken strand!

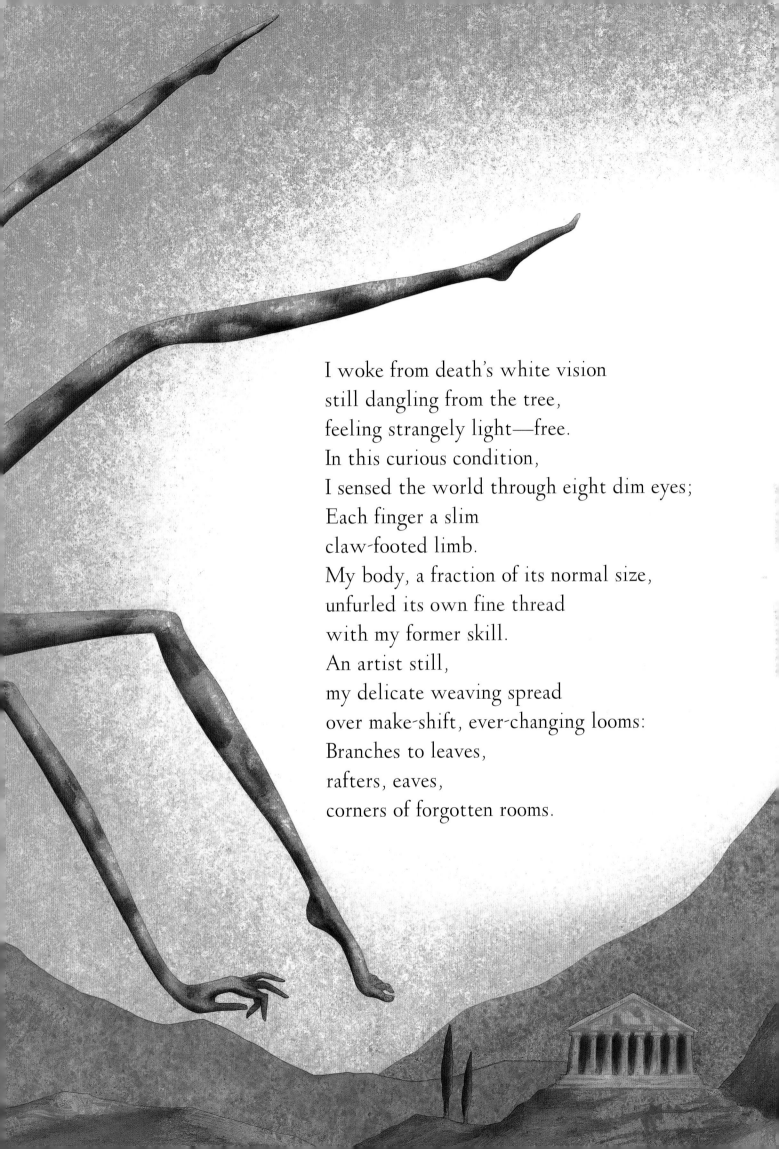

I woke from death's white vision
still dangling from the tree,
feeling strangely light—free.
In this curious condition,
I sensed the world through eight dim eyes;
Each finger a slim
claw-footed limb.
My body, a fraction of its normal size,
unfurled its own fine thread
with my former skill.
An artist still,
my delicate weaving spread
over make-shift, ever-changing looms:
Branches to leaves,
rafters, eaves,
corners of forgotten rooms.

Blown on ceaseless winds,
my thread uncurled
round a changing world.
Now, hosts of artisans
spin on in Arachne's name.
Athena, on her throne,
languishes alone,
still envying my fame.
What good is her immortality?
No incense burns
in the Parthenon's urns!
She faces cold reality
while my descendants thrive,
weaving our story again and again,
to the planet's end—
even then, we will survive.

APPENDIX

APOLLO: Greek and Roman god of the sun, also called *Phoebus*. Son of Zeus and Leto and twin brother of Artemis (Roman, *Diana*), Apollo is the patron of art, music, and medicine. He was pictured in Arachne's tapestry.

ARACHNE: Talented young weaver who refused to give credit to Athena, the patron goddess of weaving, for her accomplishments. Instead, she challenged the goddess to a weaving contest. Arachne's tapestry was flawless, but the subject matter was highly insulting to the gods. In her anger, Athena destroyed the tapestry and struck the girl. Arachne tried to hang herself, but at the last minute Athena changed her into a spider.

ATHENA (Roman, *Minerva*): Warrior goddess of wisdom and patroness of useful arts, also called *Pallas Athene*. She is said to have sprung from Zeus's head in full armor, clutching her spear and uttering a fierce battle cry. As the patron goddess of weaving, Athena was offended by Arachne's refusal to pay tribute to her. She appeared to the girl, disguised as an old woman, to warn her of the consequences of arrogance.

BOREAS: The North Wind, son of dawn (Eos) and the stars (Astraeus).

DIONYSUS (Roman, *Bacchus*): God of wine and fruitfulness who was pictured in Arachne's tapestry.

ERIGONE: Daughter of Icarius, a wealthy Athenian and supporter of Dionysus when the god was attempting to establish his rites in Athens. Dionysus seduced Erigone before departing from Athens and inadvertently caused Icarius's violent death. Grief-stricken, Erigone hanged herself. The story was pictured in Arachne's tapestry.

EUROPA: Daughter of the king of Tyre, a wealthy seaport in ancient Greece. Zeus disguised himself as a white bull and swam to the island of Crete with Europa on his back. The story was pictured in Arachne's tapestry.

PARTHENON: Athena's marble temple, built on the Acropolis in Athens, the city named for the goddess. It was built around 432 B.C. The Parthenon's ruins are famous as a tourist attraction today.

POSEIDON (Roman, *Neptune*): God of the sea and brother of Zeus. He was pictured in Arachne's tapestry.

ZEUS (Roman, *Jupiter* or *Jove*): Supreme ruler of the gods who overthrew his titan forebears and established a new order on Mount Olympus. He was the father of many Olympians, including Athena. Zeus was pictured in Arachne's tapestry.